W9-BJK-595

I Love my Mom

I Love my Mom

by Caroline Bell

Fitzhenry & Whiteside

For my Mom Margaret Helen Evans
For my Son David James Bell

Fitzhenry & Whiteside Limited
195 Allstate Parkway
Markham, Ontario L3R 4T8

Designed by Word & Image/Sandi Meland

Canadian Cataloguing in Publication Data
Bell, Caroline, 1953-
  I love my mom

ISBN 0-88902-292-5

I. Title.

PS8553.E454115 1987   JC813'.54   C87-093723-5
PZ7.B45115 1987

I love my mom
because...

She wakes me in the morning with a smile
and a hug.

She gives me a boost when I'm going slow.

She makes sure I do the things that are
good for me.

She worries if I'm late.

She protects me from danger.

She takes care of me when I have a cold.

She helps me clean up my messes.

She is understanding when I make mistakes.

She points out pretty things I might miss.

She encourages me when I think I can't.

She thinks I'm beautiful inside and out.

She believes in me when no one else does.

She is always happy to see me.

She listens when I need to talk.

She reads me a story when I'm tucked in at night.

She helps me grow into a caring person.

But Best reason of all
BECAUSE SHE LOVES ME.

Printed and bound in Hong Kong by
Wing King Tong Co., Ltd.